A HARVEST TENFOLD

Bahr Burr

A Harvest Tenfold
Bahr Burr

Copyright © 2024 by Bahr Burr
First edition, December 2024
Published by HJB Press

 HJB PRESS

Houston, TX

Editing: Erika Steeves
Formatting: Heddon Publishing
Cover illustration: Catherine Clarke Design

ISBN: 979-8-9891777-2-1 (paperback); 979-8-9891777-3-8 (ebook)
Library of Congress Control Number: 2024918790

For
tyrants everywhere,
the fools who support them,
and the cowards who tolerate them

They shout 'a hundred million heads'; that may be only a metaphor; but why be afraid of it . . .
—Dostoevsky, *Demons*

Chapter One

BILLIE SHRIEKED AGAIN, LOUDER THIS TIME.

"Stop that!" barked the emptiness staring down at her.

More of a murmur, perhaps, than a bark. Who could tell. The unctuous snarl came not through lips but from within the thing's face—if you could call it a face—stretched across the front of its amorphous head—if you could call it a head. No facial movement accompanied the sound. No eyes blinked—for there were none—and no mouth moved. A nose was an impossibility.

Yet the thick, oily voice had still oozed its way into her soul like some audibly gelatinous ichor.

"I'm sorry."

The words escaped almost involuntarily. She hadn't meant to apologize.

She tried to free her throbbing finger from its grip, but quickly realized this was impossible and changed tactics.

"Please let go! I can't do my work right if my hand is injured."

She fought back tears and stared up at the fleshy void above her. Her finger was certainly broken.

The face peered closer, as though intently scrutinizing her with phantom eyes. Billie finally understood and blurted her line.

"Hail, Despot!"

"Tremble, slave!" it gurgled back.

"Paradise on earth."

"Equality in slavery."

Its responses given, the form relaxed its grip. Billie fled up the empty street, her tortured finger pressed to her pursed lips.

***

"You're late."

"I know. A Smug stopped me."

Stan paused. "Why?"

"I don't know. I hadn't done anything."

"If it stopped you, that means you did something."

"No."

"Don't talk like that—it's dangerous! And what's wrong with your finger?"

"It broke it . . . for no reason," Billie almost wailed. She struggled to regain control, but Stan had little patience.

"Shut up!" he hissed. "Hopefully no one's listening. And where's your friend?"

"Aurora left early—she closed her finger in a door and needed medical attention." Billie managed to giggle. "At least mine wasn't so stupid."

"And that explains it," Stan snapped.

"What?"

"Your finger, and why the Smug stopped you. You should have left Aurora the moment she hurt herself."

"I tried, but she looked so sad that I couldn't leave her. She was just walking away when it approached."

Billie rubbed her close-cropped head as though to shake off the memory. Her hand now wet with the perspiration that glistened on her fuzzy scalp, she wiped it on her pants and looked timidly at Stan.

"You're not mad, are you?"

He didn't respond, but instead looked intently at the spot she'd just been rubbing. His gaze narrowed, and a distant expression came into his eyes.

"Don't say anything," Billie pleaded.

"I didn't."

"Your eyes did. I know you miss the hair, but there's nothing I can do about it."

"I know." Stan's voice softened. "I know."

His wistful gaze briefly met her brilliant yellow eyes. Sensing his tenderness, Billie wondered if she should tell him now, but her thoughts were interrupted.

"You'd better wrap it up for now. Just make sure to take off the bandage by tomorrow."

"Okay."

Chapter Two

THE CLANGING RESOUNDED TO THE INNERMOST PARTS OF her being. When it felt like every bone would crack, Billie rolled off her cot and stared panic-stricken at the blank wall.

She waited. Five seconds later, the pealing ceased.

Trembling from the close call, she hastened to get ready. Something must be wrong—she'd never been that late before. Except once, but that was enough.

Her thoughts were cut short as the loudspeaker now gave vent to a human voice.

"A harvest tenfold! All shall share in the bounty! To work—a harvest tenfold awaits!"

Work. The word sounded wrong, as though it had meant something else a long time ago. Or was it a long time? She hated this feeling—the feeling that behind a dense fog of confusion there lurked another lifetime when things had been different. It made her feel crazy. Even Stan denied it, but she knew. She'd seen him react to comments made about vague, dreamlike memories that came to her from time to time. She'd seen him stare off into nothingness with eyes that saw . . . *something.* No, she wasn't crazy. But she would be—soon. Billie felt sure of this and shuddered as she ate her allotted rations.

Ten minutes later, she was dressed in her loose brown cotton pants and work shirt, the standard uniform of the day.

They used to have different uniforms for different days, but then days no longer had names, just numbers. Then the numbers went away, since some numbers are higher than others, and every day was Day 1. But 1 implied primacy, so now every day was Day 0, and every day was nothing and all the uniforms were the same color. It annoyed Billie at first—she missed the brighter colors. But keeping track was hard, and wearing the same thing every day was easier, just like they'd promised.

Billie flew down the several flights of stairs and into the brilliantly lit street. She glanced over her shoulder at the hateful facade glaring down at her and all the other workers emerging from its humming bowels. She feared this place—this grim shell that released its inhabitants with reluctance every morning and gathered them into its concrete embrace each night like a jealous, breeze-block lover. She feared and hated all its problems, the most recent being a lack of hot shower water. The chirpy building overseer had assured her yesterday that he'd see to it right away.

"Hey!"

Billie turned her head slightly at the whispered voice but kept walking, her sore finger pressed against a stomach which now churned every morning with wave after wave of nausea.

"Hey."

"Did you hear the rumor?" Zora queried.

"Which one?"

"About the demolition."

"I don't understand." Billie glanced around nervously. "Don't slow down. And talk quieter."

"I heard we're going to be moved. Our building is one of the very last to go."

"I hope not," Billie murmured. "It's terrible, but at least we still have our own rooms, unlike everyone else."

"Well, it's going to happen," Zora returned, bobbing her head excitedly. "I'm glad—I didn't feel right, although I'm only on the second stage. I can't imagine how you feel, all high and mighty up there on stage four! The new ones don't have stages—they're just one continuous stage that takes up a whole block. How cool is that!"

Billie looked at her friend in disgust but kept moving.

"Oh, can I use your shower tonight? And tomorrow, maybe?" Zora asked.

"Why?"

"My hot water won't work for some reason."

Billie paused momentarily before hurrying on, leaving her bemused neighbor behind.

***

She arrived panting, her head pounding and a feeling of panic almost overwhelming her.

It was strange. Why was she surprised? Hadn't things always been like this? She made her way to her assigned station, blinking in the stunning glow of the overhead lights. Every day her head hurt, and the lights made it worse. And was it her imagination, or were they really getting brighter? Brighter, and the booming loudspeakers louder.

Suddenly, the loudspeakers in question crackled to life. Every uniformed worker snapped to attention, staring straight ahead.

The voice spoke.

"By order of the Grand Despot, by whose benevolence all enjoy the luxuries of an existence devoid of feelings and boredom—characteristics of aristocratic societies not befitting an enlightened despotism—a statement will now be made concerning the further implementation of the leveling measures guiding the development of this paradisical system. Slogan Thirteen!"

All responded: "Only the necessary is necessary!"

Billie and her colleagues belted out this response with almost no facial movements, their harsh voices raking the vast building's rough walls like automatic gunfire.

"Only the necessary is necessary," affirmed the loudspeakers. "But much which is not necessary remains, due to the infancy of this glorious program. Names, for example. These are not necessary."

Billie winced.

"By order of the Grand Despot, no worker shall have a name! Names are property, and desire for property springs from familial relationships which have already been abolished. In addition, names destroy equality and can no longer be tolerated, as they elevate some slaves over others. Slogan Nine!"

"Reduce all to a common denominator!"

"And thus," the buoyant voice continued, "all shall now share the name of SLAVE! All share and share alike! Under this title only shall you address and be addressed. And how shall you distinguish, you ask?" The voice positively squealed with delight. "How shall you distinguish? You won't, of course! Distinguishing is, by definition, an exclusion, and all exclusions subvert equality. We don't distinguish days—why should we persons? You are nothingness. You are one solid mass granted freedom from the oppressive burden of individuality and its disparity in genius. You are free—freed by complete despotism which unites all and prefers none! A system which will reap a harvest . . . a harvest—"

"Ten-fold! Ten-fold! Ten-fold!"

The building shook with the reverberating intonation. Billie, chanting like all the rest, glanced down the endless, towering vestibule at the monolithic workers yelling themselves hoarse, their rough boots stomping in unison. She felt sick. How could they all go on chanting, perfectly content? Didn't they care—didn't they feel a hopeless impotence welling up inside them as their identities were erased? Stifling a desire to scream in rage at the nearest automaton, she listened as the chanting died down and the Anthem played. The loudspeakers now silent, she could begin her work.

"Greetings, slave," she murmured to the form next to her.

Chapter Three

MORANA YAWNED AND STRETCHED HER CRAMPED NECK. A head poked in the open doorway.

"You done? Everyone else left." Cozbi tapped her foot impatiently.

"Since when do you come down here?" Morana asked, surprised by her friend's presence.

"Since they decided to cart the birthers up here instead of dealing with them in the Enclosure, like they should. Better facilities here, I guess. I still don't know how you manage. Why do we need them, anyway? I once heard someone say we should just get rid of the Herd and run everything on scientific principles."

"I've heard that too," Morana replied, pulling off her rubber gloves. "It won't work, apparently. Still . . . it sure sounds nice. No more testing . . . no more leveling . . ."

"How many did you do today?"

"A few dozen. It's normally about a hundred new offspring a day that come through and on average a third of them require leveling."

"See, that's what I mean!" Cozbi said. "Just let them die off!"

"They say it's impossible," Morana pursued doggedly. "I don't really know. Let's talk about something else."

Cozbi smirked. "Like your boyfriend? I saw him this morning—chest stuck out like some hero just because he's been assigned to the Shock squad. Barely even said hi to me!"

"His work is important."

"It is, but not so important he can't say hello to an old friend."

Morana winced. More like an old lover. Her beauty was unmatched, but Cozbi's higher rank might seduce Drake again. Cozbi had correctly analyzed Drake's character as valuing status above all else. Morana still loved him, though, even when he made her suffer.

She trudged down the street, her friend jouncing along beside her. Why must she chatter so? Morana's thoughts trailed back to one she'd leveled that morning. Really smart. Passed every test with flying colors, though just short of genius level, *thankfully*. Morana shuddered. Why was she sympathizing with the Herd? Why with the birther standing there, anxiously watching the testing as though her life depended on it? Not hers perhaps, but certainly his. Ten points higher and he's a goner. As it was, Morana had whisked him off to the Oscillation Room for the proper amount of treatment. His birther would see him again, but he wouldn't be the same.

"And then there's the face," continued Cozbi. "Remember when Smugs had normal faces?"

"No," murmured Morana, trying to clear her confused brain. "I mean, yeah . . . I think so. But what does that have to do with anything?"

"You goose!" Cozbi tittered. "You weren't even listening! I was just saying we should have better science by this point. Remember ages ago when they told us we'd figure out how to live forever? Or make everyone super smart? And now we're still dying like before and making offspring dumber on purpose."

"Only Herd offspring, though."

"Of course only Herd offspring! Tithers have always been exempt. But I was saying how my department makes the Smugs. It's not nearly as complicated as everyone thinks. We don't have the means to do anything complicated—if we did, you'd be out of a job."

"I know." Morana grasped her head with both hands and stopped walking. Cozbi glanced at her curiously.

"Hurting again? Maybe try to get some quiet."

"Thanks, I will."

"Where are you going?"

"I . . . don't remember."

Cozbi grinned slyly. "Let's go to the Enclosure then."

"Why?"

"Maybe the noise will make your headache go away. You clearly don't have anything more important to do."

Morana shook her head but followed her friend obediently. She tried to breathe and enjoy the fresh scent of the trees lining their course. The road, impressively broad and straight as an arrow, sloped downward at a perfectly consistent gradient which made travel easy for those who chose to walk.

The massive open gates loomed before them as they reached the bottom of the interminable hill. The wall stood ten times their height, its shining facade searing their eyes as the late afternoon sun struck its brushed metallic surface. The sentry waved them through. As they climbed the main tower, Cozbi extolled the malleable simplicity of the guard captain who allowed her visits. Emerging onto the watch platform, she cast an alluring smile at the subject of her prattling discourse and beckoned him over from his observation post.

"You've come to watch the Levelers again?" he asked, grinning.

"Yes!" Cozbi commandeered the proffered telescope without any hesitation. "Oh, they've got a lot done!" she cooed as she directed her enhanced gaze toward a spot far in the distance.

The captain, eager to impress, nodded in agreement.

"Yes! I have it on good authority that the buildings will be finished soon. The hills will take longer, but not many more need to go."

Cozbi moved aside and motioned Morana over. "Take a look."

Morana settled herself behind the telescope and scanned the entire vista before her. An immense plateau, perfectly level, stretched for miles. The wall shot out like an enormous *V* from the gated vertex where she stood. A drab sea of uniformly constructed buildings stretched endlessly toward a low, distant mountain range that arced from wall to wall and transformed the entire area into a massive, sunbaked slice of concrete pie. In the center of this homogeneous infinity stood the Spire, a towering monolith and observation point. Moving among this dreary blockscape Morana observed Leveling crews removing any residual greenery that provided some relief from the glaring sun. Distant explosions marked the demolition of the few remaining multilevel structures, leaving only the massive bulk of the great Work Hall—visible to the naked eye even from this distance—untouched. As Morana peered closely through the telescope, a rumbling far deeper and more menacing shook the earth as dust completely obscured a distant hill.

"They sure pack a punch, those large charges!" the captain quipped.

"What a waste!" Morana murmured. The captain looked at her in surprise.

"A waste? Why would you say that?"

"They could build on those foothills—they're not even as steep as the one we just walked down. And yet they blow them to bits."

The captain regarded her suspiciously. "Don't you know the Anthem? And the Herd slogans? Number Two, in particular?"

"Level the mountains!" Cozbi sang in a playful voice. "Don't mind her—she's just grumpy, that's all." She began flirting with the captain, leaving Morana to her own thoughts.

Level the mountains. Morana shook her head. Damn the slogans! And the Anthem, even if it fascinated her. They'd be playing it soon. Turning to find her friend still engaged, she slipped away and headed home.

***

Morana found Drake waiting for her, a condescending grin besmirching an otherwise handsome face. Bracing herself for a burst of anger, she instead received worse.

"Ah, there she is—the queen of the dregs! The ally of the filth and friend of the scum! Why, if only I was a slave so I could receive your majesty's gracious benevolence and pity!"

"What do you mean?" Morana asked, hurt by her lover's biting tone.

"I've been informed"—Drake raised one eyebrow knowingly—"that our favorite offspring Leveler feels sorry for the nasty little things! Everyone in your department is talking about it—says you can hardly bring yourself to do your job. Now, I can't have that, not when my reputation is on the line! And why do you care about them anyway?"

"I don't!" Morana faltered. "I mean, not enough to . . . I still do my job! Who's been reporting me?" Her exaggerated anger betrayed underlying fear.

"It's their duty," Drake replied, eyeing her ironically. "You think the Calumny Bureau limits itself to Herd activities? That's its main function, but there's also a division for Tither sedition. Anyone suspected of empathy toward the Herd gets reported, plain and simple. Tempest told me all about it."

Morana tossed her head with feigned indifference.

"Tempest is a show-off. If all I did was process reports from Herd spies all day I'd go crazy, and the fact that she's fine with it means she's got no ambition."

"And what are your ambitions?" Drake's penetrating gaze unsettled her.

"I don't have any."

"No? And here you are, mocking Tempest for just that!"

"Oh . . . I meant that she's bad at her job and doesn't care to get better. I'm always seeking to improve."

"Not according to your coworkers," Drake replied. "You *can* be good at your job, I'll give you that. Not that your job is all that hard. If you ever want to match Cozbi or even reach my level, you'll need to dispense with any emotions toward those things you handle. Take my advice—I want to help you."

He patted her on the head, and she smiled weakly.

"You shouldn't be mad at me," she ventured. "It's not that I care about slaves, exactly . . . It's just hard to separate things. You know I want a baby, and that makes me see them differently."

Drake frowned menacingly.

"Enough! We've talked too much about this—I told you it's not going to happen!"

"But it's our duty! You're the one always talking about our obligations to the System!"

"No! It's the Herd's duty, albeit under strict parameters. Tithers aren't required to reproduce—we can get all the offspring we want from the Herd, although that takes effort."

"You wouldn't mind that kind of effort!" Morana retorted bitterly.

Drake stared hard at her.

"Sleeping with Herd birthers is acceptable. I don't—I consider it beneath me—but doing so is not against System principles. Superintendent Dorg even advocates it."

"Dorg is a monster!" Morana countered, shuddering. "And if you work for him long enough you'll become just like him."

"He asked about you the other day," Drake responded, ignoring her gibe. "Asked where 'that pretty little playmate' of mine was. That's a good way of putting it too." Drake laughed.

"Aren't I more than just a playmate?" Morana asked timidly.

Drake shrugged. "You're pretty clever—far too clever for such a low-level position, if only you'd align yourself properly with System principles. But I didn't come here to discuss that."

"No?" Morana brightened.

"No. I have important news—I've been placed on the Shock squad."

"I know." Morana tried to look excited. "I'm proud of you."

"And now that I have a new role, things will be different around here. I'm afraid I can't be sharing secrets with someone of lower rank, especially one whose loyalty is . . . suspect. I also can't be seen as often with you. Not much at all, in fact."

"Why not?" Morana tried not to panic but her voice betrayed desperation.

"It's not proper. You're a hindrance to my career. I'll still stop by—discreetly, of course—when I need something, but that's it."

When he needs something. Morana bit her tongue and fought back tears. She knew what he'd need, but no baby would come from it. *That* feeling was coming back now—that vague impression, that desperate longing. For what, though? A child? Yes, that was always there, but it was something more, something vast. But she could never figure out what exactly.

The door slammed. Drake had left without even saying goodbye. Morana slumped into a heap on the floor and burst into tears.

Chapter Four

THE BITING WIND CUT THROUGH BILLIE'S THIN UNIFORM like a thousand frigid scalpels. She moaned softly and clutched her mutilated chest with both arms, exacerbating the searing pain from her recent surgery.

Surgery. More like butchery. All of them, one after the other, like chattel. And the crudeness of it all. The fact that they hadn't even noticed her condition proved their barbaric sloppiness. It was better that way, though. She still had hope. In what, she didn't know, but as her own weak frame crumbled, the life growing inside her strengthened her resolve to survive. They hadn't noticed! But they would, and soon.

She staggered through the large doors toward her station as though in a dream, trying not to scream as the jostling of hundreds of bodies sent jolts of pain throughout her entire body. The seething mass of mute humanity flowed through the gaping halls in one homogeneous blob of pale flesh. She shuddered as she passed a Harvester who stood scrutinizing the passing horde. It was him again—the one with the pale eyes. She could feel those eyes boring into her soul at this very moment, even as she took her place and stood like a statue while the Anthem played. Why was he staring at her? She felt a desperate urge to cover her midsection but remained still until work provided welcome relief.

She felt a hand on her shoulder.

"Slave!"

The command lacked instructions, but it was a command, nonetheless. Billie started and cast a despairing look at the Harvester's pallid eyes. It was strange. No fury, no hate. Not even the cold impassivity typifying his kind. Only an earnestness that completely baffled her.

Billie obediently followed the Harvester. She had always imagined it would be different—that she'd refuse to go silently, like her former friends. What cowards they were! She'd always despised them, and now she would meet her end in the same manner.

They walked for a full ten minutes, passing from the enormous open vestibule with its hundreds of living corpses to private hallways leading past grim-looking offices until they finally reached a series of small, unoccupied rooms deep in the bowels of this gigantic building. The Harvester opened a door marked *Threshing 1* and pulled Billie inside.

They were alone.

Chapter Five

HE FINISHED COMBING HIS THIN HAIR AND ADJUSTED HIS plain tie. Staring at the wan figure in the mirror, he shook his head slightly. The salt-and-pepper hair was ever thinner, the face ever paler. He missed the thin mustache which had imparted a look of distinction and dignified authority to an otherwise unimpressive face. He had never abused that authority. Those who taught should have authority, if only to authorize free thinking. But that was some time ago. Now, he looked and felt old, and Harvesters must be clean-shaven. But nobody could prevent his dressing up for a private dinner, especially one without guests.

His toilet complete, he entered the tiny dining area and carefully laid an ancient though immaculate cloth on the small table, followed by two finely engraved porcelain plates, two sets of pewter flatware, and two crystal wine glasses, one of which he filled. Disappearing into the dimly lit kitchenette, he re-emerged carrying a tray with a small cutlet, a slice of which he placed on the nearest plate. Some artichokes followed, along with a small baked potato tastefully garnished and bathed in butter. He hesitated and looked at the bare plate. No. This was her night, but she wasn't here, and there was no point in carrying the ritual that far. She wouldn't approve. Simply setting an extra place was sufficient.

He glanced around the tiny cupboard of a room, taking in

the bare walls, the threadbare carpet, and the tiny window placed precisely at a height conducive neither to seated nor standing viewing. This small aperture, barely larger than a shoebox, had a sliding panel that opened halfway. That would be enough. He reached over, threw the latch, and slid the thin sheet of glass aside. He then checked his watch and positioned himself before the open window, back straight, his weight leaning forward on a slightly bent leg, hands clasped against a simple waistcoat.

The Anthem began, the first instrumental sounds wafting through the garret window with surprising clearness.

And now the listener sang. He sang with a magnificent tenor voice which perfectly matched the distant music. Sang with such depth of feeling that tears streamed down his face, forming tiny blots on the otherwise spotless carpet. Sang until the music ceased and silence prevailed.

He wiped his cheeks with a pocket handkerchief, closed the window, and sat down. He inclined his head, remaining perfectly still for several seconds, then looked up and eagerly seized his full glass. Raising it to the empty space before him, he smiled tenderly.

***

The meal over, he sat thinking, the empty dishes still before him and the gathering darkness casting gloomy shadows on the walls.

Tomorrow. She was the right one. He knew she was pregnant. It wasn't yet visible, but he still knew. Everything—her face, her movements, the expression in her frightened eyes—gave her away. He'd been doing this long enough to notice things others missed. Too long, perhaps. He had needed time to plan, but at what point did inaction become complicity? How many had he harvested while planning his little revolt? Should he have just refused from the start? He'd have been harvested himself, thus destroying the plan germinating in his mind ever since his wife's demise. But his conscience would have been clean. Which was better: sin as you work to save humanity or remain virtuous and lose the chance to eradicate the evil permanently? He didn't know. But back to that slave. She was desperate—he could tell. It had become especially noticeable the day fellow Harvesters had taken her lover. For what, he didn't remember. Not for being her lover, a secret only he had deduced. He knew lots of secrets, and the fact that he kept them secret encouraged him. He wasn't fully corrupted.

Yes, tomorrow he'd do it. He wanted to help her, and she'd be able to help him. His decision made, he rose and began clearing the dishes.

Chapter Six

BILLIE CAST HER EYES AROUND THE SMALL ROOM. THERE was nothing but a desk with a chair behind it and lights so bright they made her wince.

As the Harvester closed the door, she planted herself in front of the desk with her hands clasped over her stomach like a protective shield. To her intense surprise, the Harvester took her by the shoulders and pushed her behind the desk and into the chair. Her tense body collapsed as the Harvester assumed her former position.

"It's Billie, isn't it?"

Billie shuddered. "What? I mean . . . pardon?"

"Your name's Billie, right?"

Billie felt her entire body start shaking. She completely lost her head.

"The Harvest is near—Slogan One!" she wailed. "Level the mountains—Slogan Two! Slaves must—"

"Silence!" The Harvester brought his fist down on the table. Billie froze.

"I'm sorry . . . I can't stand the slogans." His voice was strangely soft. "I can't stand them. But I was asking your name."

Billie trembled. "I don't have a name. I'm a slave. I'm not even an *I*, but I don't know how else to express it. We're all slaves, all of us. Not you, of course . . . I mean my fellow slaves. Of course,

22

they're not *mine*, because *I* don't exist as such, but . . ."

Her babbling trailed off into nothingness. The Harvester regarded her silently.

"Your name *is* Billie—I looked it up. Mine's Barney. And we're two people, two *individuals*, having a little talk."

Billie's mind reeled. What was this? He was saying things contrary to everything she'd been taught. Was it a trap? Undoubtedly, but Billie suddenly realized she had nothing to lose.

"I . . . don't remember," she faltered, quite honestly. She had forgotten, if only momentarily. Everything started flooding back, and she grew a trifle bolder.

"No, you're right, Despot. I remember now."

"It's Barney—don't call me Despot. Despot means tyrant. Barney means something different."

"What?" Billie queried, surprised at her own temerity.

Barney paused and regarded her thoughtfully. "It's a nickname, really—one I got when I was younger. It means encourager, or consoler."

Billie stared blankly.

"How many months is it now?" Barney asked softly.

"How many what?"

"Months. Or . . . how long . . . that is, when will you give birth?"

Billie almost screamed. All concern for her own well-being instantly vanished.

"Don't take him—please!" she cried. "I know I was never assigned a mating role, but it was before the mandate—I swear! Just before—and before they took him . . . the father, that is. Don't take him too! I'll do anything, anything! Just let me give birth—you can change the records and say I had an assignment! Make it official! Please! . . ."

Sobs choked her voice.

"How do you know it's a boy? Do you even remember what a boy is?" Barney asked. "The Herd has no such distinctions—all are equal. Your surgery reflects that."

"I remember," Billie sobbed. "And I just know it's a boy."

"And how will you manage? Where will you hide it, and how will you feed it? Certainly not with what they give you."

"I don't know!" Billie moaned. "I can't think that far ahead. All I know is that I must keep him."

She leaned forward on the desk and buried her face in her hands. The Harvester watched her closely.

"Yes, I agree—it's a boy," he began. "And I think he'll be an important one . . . for many reasons. I want to save him."

Billie raised her head. "Really?"

"Yes. And you—both of you."

"You care about us?"

"Yes, I do. But there are other reasons. Selfish ones—I want that made clear. I need you for a very dangerous project, but one which will hopefully save many others."

"I'll help."

"Wait. My saving your child is not dependent on your assisting me. Is that clear?"

Billie nodded. "Yes, but I'll still help."

"Even though it's dangerous?"

Billie smiled bitterly. "Yes. Danger means nothing to me anymore."

"Okay," the Harvester responded, clearly pleased. "We need to plan."

Chapter Seven

DORG HAD A PERFECT FACE. TOO PERFECT, MORANA thought. The brilliant sapphire eyes held sway over everything beneath their gaze. A graceful brow sat like a chiseled nimbus above a fine nose and a sensuous mouth enclosing two perfect rows of pearly white teeth. The ivory skin shone with a brilliant, angelic radiance. The fine hair—its short, supple curls combed back and quaffed into a subtle mane—showed no hint of gray despite its bearer's six decades of life. No wrinkles marred this visage—no blemishes its purity.

It sat atop a lithe, wiry form cosseted in a luxurious suit which moved with such sinuous dexterity upon its owner that it gave the impression of a royal blue serpent sashaying forward on its hindmost parts, its head raised and poised to strike. Morana felt even now like a helpless creature petrified by the cobra's hypnotic leer. She tried to disengage her eyes from his, but some horrible fascination held her gaze. Dorg smiled.

"Ms. Morana! Welcome!"

The slight drawl with its velvety tones struck Morana as a strange combination. She knew Dorg only by reputation, one which was not conducive to further inquiry.

"Hello, sir."

"And why is your sweet face showing itself in my office?"

"You sent for me, sir," Morana began, growing confused.

"At least, that's what I was told, but I've been rather confused lately."

"I'm aware—Drake told me." Dorg smiled at Morana's surprised look. "Yes, Ms. Morana—I know all about it. Drake tells me everything, and you're going to do the same."

"Yes, sir."

Dorg checked his watch and rose from behind his enormous desk. "The evening Anthem, Ms. Morana."

Morana remained motionless until the discreet office speakers faded into silence. Looking for truthful points of agreement, she decided to praise the music.

"I like the melody, sir—it's so beautiful."

"It's a wonderful piece!" Dorg agreed as he reseated himself. "It was composed specifically for the System."

"I've heard it before."

"Of course." Dorg smiled again.

"No, sir . . . I mean I heard it a long time ago . . . before all *this*, but I can't remember where."

Morana instantly regretted this revelation. Dorg's eyes narrowed to tiny slits, his entire face contracting with such intense concentration that the perfect mouth disappeared into a tiny oval of pursed whiteness. She almost expected a long flickering tongue to shoot forth. The eyes gleamed.

"I trust, Ms. Morana, that you speak in jest. I happen to know the artist in question—a most talented individual— who composed and sang the Anthem by personal request of the Grand Despot. And what could you possibly mean by *this*?"

"Oh, just . . . everything as we now know it." Morana could feel drops of sweat collecting on her flushed brow.

"Everything as we now know it." Dorg seemed to roll the

words around in his mouth as though determining their veracity by taste. "But my dear girl, that implies things were at some point different, no?"

"I don't . . . know," Morana faltered. "I don't really know what I meant. I'm probably wrong about the Anthem too . . . *definitely* wrong, sir, if you know where it comes from. I just thought I'd heard it a long time ago, and since I couldn't remember where, I assumed it was someplace else, but I was wrong." Morana, visibly shaking at this point, cursed herself for these blatant lies which poured forth under the Superintendent's terrible gaze.

"That's what I thought," Dorg said, his facial expression relaxing into one of beaming satisfaction, though the fire remained in his eyes. "Of course, your key mistake was in doubting yourself. You know where the Anthem comes from—you always knew. You just didn't know that you knew, but now that you are aware of your knowledge, that knowledge makes itself known. All it takes to know is to know that you know what you always knew!"

Morana regarded him uneasily, unsure whether to take this lecture seriously or as a mocking reprimand. She decided to take the safe approach and merely inclined her head ambiguously. Dorg continued.

"Your next mistake was framing your argument in the context of time. What is time? Time has been erased for the Herd—they no longer need it, as it only exacerbates feelings of inequality we've worked so hard to eliminate. You know all this, my dear. You also know that we Tithers must still endure a yoke which the Herd have cast off—a yoke of desires. The Herd have no desires, therefore they do not suffer. Tithers have desires, and therefore suffer accordingly, and these sufferings are marked by time, for they are not permanent. And if they are not permanent, that means they come and go over time, so you see that time—for the Tither—is indeed necessary. But time is not something over which to rejoice, for it is a burden we must carry. Slaves must have Directors, as Slogan Three makes clear, but those Directors must take upon themselves the burdens of directorship. It is a sacrifice made for the nine-tenths of society who now experience complete despotism and the perfect freedom it engenders. A sacrifice which makes Directors like you and me—the other tenth, the sacrificial Tithe—subject to the encumbering concept of time which hangs round our necks like a giant millstone. And yet, you seem to view time as beneficial—a most subversive concept! Your reference to a *past* of sorts implies an actual *desire* for time rather than stoic acceptance of a sacrificial burden you must bear. Must *bear*, Ms. Morana!"

Morana nodded vigorously.

"All Tithers have their own burdens to bear and roles to perform. Harvesters must harvest, Smugs enforce, and Levelers level. And that leads us right back to where we started—your situation, and how you were going to tell me everything. In short, you are here to explain to me why your performance is not meeting standards."

"I'm not sure which standards you're referring to, sir," Morana began. "My work at the offspring leveling center hasn't really changed, even after the Herd policies did. I don't understand all the high-level stuff, sir, but I do know that my orders remained the same."

"Of course they did," Dorg snapped. "And it's not your job

to analyze your orders, but I see an explanation is necessary." The Superintendent leaned back in his ornately carved chair, folded his hands behind his upturned head, and began speaking in an earnest, yet dreamy voice with his eyes half-closed.

"The Herd is necessary, Ms. Morana. Many people have wondered why this is the case. Your friend Cozbi, for example, though she outranks you, has raised questions. She is spared for her simplicity—a simplicity marked by extreme devotedness to the System. You, my good girl, defended the principle I am about to expound, though perhaps with insidious motives for doing so.

"You seem to feel the Herd is necessary simply out of empathy. In other words, you feel sorry for them and don't want them all harvested. This is selfishness, pure and simple. You operate not out of compassion but out of venal laziness, a desire to avoid the burdens of directorship I just mentioned. You might try to convince yourself of altruistic motives, but at heart you know this not to be the case.

"The Herd is necessary, and why is it necessary? Numbers, Ms. Morana—numbers dictate that it must be so. There are billions of people on this planet—far too many to simply harvest and be done with them all, even with countless other Threshing Centers worldwide operating in unison as we speak. The notion that the entire Herd should be harvested, leaving only a remnant—the educated, or those we now call Directors or Tithers—to live scientifically henceforth without burden or hindrance is indeed a most fascinating and appealing concept, but one which is impractical if not actually impossible. This was determined some time ago by Directors of the highest rank, intelligence, and scientific pedigree. The Herd are certainly tame, but they remain a threat if for no other reason than their staggering superiority in numbers. Attempts to harvest them all would certainly provoke an eventual backlash of gargantuan proportions. No, better to harvest a modest number—say, a tenfold increase from the previous century, comprised of the exceptional members who cannot be leveled, and thus remove the main impediments to the universal equality for which we strive. For perfect freedom to exist, a system of total despotism must be implemented. And for this system to succeed, there must be no desires, no boredom, and constant work. Since boredom will certainly become a factor at some point despite our best efforts, we will create Shock events which will force the Herd to abandon any subversive ideas as they turn on each other instead. Drake can explain all that to you, if he hasn't already. The rest of the time, we simply rely on a system of spying, where every Herd member spies on every other, thus giving their busy little brains something with which to occupy themselves. It's working quite well, and at this point their individual identities have been virtually erased. In another few decades, they will have been re-educated to such an extent that they achieve a state of ingenuous purity, an artless simplicity of soul admitting no thought of rebellion. At that point, Ms. Morana, the earthly paradise will truly be established."

Dorg fully opened his eyes and looked steadily at Morana.

"As to your orders. You are correct—they were not changed despite the shift in policies. These things must be done gradually. Slaves were initially allowed relationships, but as we impressed upon them the dangers of individuality, a subsequent abolishment of personal ties naturally followed. You thus shifted from leveling the offspring of spouses and lovers to leveling the offspring of mandated couplings. As I just noted, instituting the paradise will take a few generations, so offspring must still be produced, but they must be produced without love, desire, or self-interest. Copulation for any reason other than System principles cannot therefore be tolerated, and that which does occur is by assignment. But this does not change your work! You are not to analyze an offspring's origins but rather to assess its potential and act accordingly. So yes, you are correct in saying your task has not changed."

Morana nodded again.

"I see you agree. The question then arises: why have your actions changed?"

"Actions, sir?"

"Your numbers are down by half."

"Not my processing numbers, sir. I've processed the exact same number I always have."

"But the number leveled is reduced to a mere fraction of previous outputs," Dorg retorted. "Why is that?"

"I didn't realize the leveling numbers had standards, sir," Morana said timidly. "I simply test them like I always have. Those with high intellects are leveled. Those with superior intellects are harvested."

"So, you're saying that recent months just happened to have fewer offspring with high intellects?"

"I . . . guess so, sir," Morana faltered. Dorg stared straight through her.

"I see. Well, let's hope so, my dear. If it were ever determined that offspring with high intellects were being overlooked, the one responsible for the overlooking would be in a most uncomfortable position."

"Yes, sir."

"That's all—you may go."

Morana bowed slightly, spun around, and fled as quickly as propriety and caution would allow.

Dorg smiled and returned to his work.

Chapter Eight

THE SHOUTS OF THE ECSTATIC CROWD MADE MORANA'S head feel like it would split at any moment. Noise and excessive heat created unbearable pain, and she only saved herself from collapsing by staggering against the bloated form standing in front of her. The figure turned.

"Aha, it's you!" he exclaimed, twisting his puffy maggot face into a hideous grin. "And here I'd given up looking for you, only to find you right behind me!" He sniggered. "Come to watch the parade?"

"Yes," Morana murmured, making no effort to hide her revulsion.

"Say, I heard that Drake dumped you. My sympathies and all that, but it's been a long time coming. Those fancy boys care too much about their prestige. I may only be a simple Harvester, but you know I'll treat you better than that."

Morana avoided his unsettling gaze.

"He didn't exactly dump me. He still sees me . . . sometimes."

The knowing grin grew wider.

"I'm sure he does! He knows a good thing when he sees it. As do I! Take, for example, the—"

"Look at all the Smugs!" interrupted Morana, pointing to a large group of Enforcers marching past, their slab faces glistening in the sunlight. She welcomed the distraction.

Grub shrugged. "Whatever. Nothing special about them,

unless you're turned on by nasal cavities. That's what you'd see underneath. They lop the nose and ears off and slap that perforated mask over the top. They use buttocks flesh for that—I know since I'm in charge of selecting the choicest samples from the Harvest."

He laughed so repulsively that Morana almost gagged.

"I'm not interested, and if I was, Cozbi could tell me all about it."

"Cozbi's no better than Drake," Grub retorted. "So full of themselves. All she does is administer the feeding cocktails, but since it's Smugs and not offspring, she ranks higher than you."

Morana remained silent. She wanted to simply disappear in the large crowd but felt too physically weak to even move. The Harvester leaned down, his face with its odor of decay mere inches from her twitching nose.

"I've waited long enough," he hissed. "Give me what I want, or I'll make trouble for you. It wouldn't be hard—I know you're already in hot water with the Superintendent."

She closed her eyes and tried holding her breath but was left gasping from her vain efforts. Her salvation arrived in the form of several other Harvesters who recognized a comrade and barged their way through the crowd toward them. There were four—all strangers—and Morana listened with relief to their boisterous discourse. They extolled the merits of the System and its special holidays, but she paid no heed until she noticed one of them quietly watching her. He was a rather insignificant-looking fellow, middle-aged, with pale eyes that seemed to search out her inmost thoughts. She shifted uncomfortably, but the eyes followed.

"Hey! Barney-puss!" shouted one of the group over the din. "Why so quiet?"

"He's always quiet!"

"Yeah, but now he's checking out that fine sample over there. Can't take his eyes off her!"

Morana shot a quick look at Grub before walking deliberately up to the quiet Harvester and loudly introducing herself with exaggerated friendliness, yet still avoiding the eyes.

"Hi—I'm Morana! I work in the offspring leveling center. I haven't seen you before!"

A murderous glance from Grub quelled her feigned enthusiasm. She quickly assumed a more reserved air as she shook the extended hand.

"Barney. Nice to meet you, Miss."

"His full name's Barnabus," said one of the others. "You can see why he's shortened it."

"With a name like that, they should shorten him instead!" joked another. "The Herd surgeons could help with that!"

The Harvester ignored his companions. "And what exactly do you do at the leveling center, Miss?"

"She levels the offspring, you shrimp! What else would she do?" Grub interrupted.

"And do you enjoy your work?" Barney queried, still addressing Morana.

"Yes."

"She's lying," Grub snarled. "She hates it, and now she's in trouble."

Barney regarded Morana thoughtfully, but a sudden shout from the gathered crowd cut short their interview. Morana looked up and saw several special formations sauntering past, clad in gaudy dress uniforms worn only on special occasions. She barely recognized Drake, but the arrogant tilt of the covered head combined with that unmistakable gait instantly revealed his presence. She waved, but he merely looked through her and continued along, a conceited smirk providing the only sign of recognition. Morana dropped her hand in despair, only to feel something pressed into it while hanging limply at her side. Before she could react, tremendous jostling from a crowd that now followed the last of the parade down the street almost knocked her over, and she had to fight to avoid being crushed from behind. Several breathless minutes later, she managed to find a sheltered shop front where she plopped down, breathing heavily. She felt sick. Only after regaining control of herself did she remember. She quickly opened her hand and peeled a rumpled scrap of paper out of her clammy palm.

The words *Be early tomorrow* were scrawled across it. She stared, not comprehending.

Be early? To work? That must be it . . . but why? And by whose orders? She shook her head. She wouldn't be early—she'd probably be late. And tired. She rose gingerly and stretched her sore limbs. It was time to head home and to early bed.

*****

Barney was waiting for her when she arrived.

"I thought you'd come."

"I almost didn't. I thought it might be a trap." Morana instantly regretted her compromising admission.

"Trap?"

"Uh, yeah . . . from Grub. He harasses me."

"Grub can barely write. But there's something more. You're afraid."

"Me?" Morana's forced laugh echoed harshly off the bare lab walls. "What am I afraid of?"

"The System, and those who run it. I know your background, Miss—I've heard it from others, and I've done my own research as well. I'm good at collecting information, especially with regards to a kindred spirit."

"Kindred spirit?"

"Yes—we both hate the System. Don't argue," he ordered, seeing her intent to reply. "This isn't the trap you feared. I want to bring the System down forever. I'm compromising myself to gain your trust. If you wanted to get back in their good graces, all you'd need to do is say you've discovered a massive plot. You'd be a hero."

Morana stared at him. The truth of his words hit her so forcefully that she almost laughed aloud. He was right! Instantly she'd be promoted from this low-level position to one of rank and prestige. Dorg would commend her—Drake would fall on his knees and beg her forgiveness. She'd slap Grub's bulbous face, ignore Cozbi altogether, and send that backstabbing spy Tempest packing. And all the coworkers who envied her beauty and reported her. All of them! She'd reign supreme over the whole System! One which she hated.

No. It didn't matter. Nothing mattered. She'd tried to hit normal numbers this past week, even leveling a few too many in her burst of zeal, but she couldn't do it anymore. She looked at Barney.

"But you won't do that," he said quietly. "I can judge a person well, and you won't report me. I need your help."

"With what?"

Barney smiled. "Today you'll receive a visitor. Her name won't be on any of your lists, but treat her as if she is. I'll take care of the rest."

And with that, he was gone.

***

The visitor arrived as promised, shortly before closing time. Morana recognized her immediately by the strange, almost unearthly gaze of mingled terror and hope this wasted young creature cast upon her. She had never seen a look of such acute suffering and despair, yet the intensity of the yearning in her eyes betrayed faith in services Morana felt unsure she'd be able to provide. How would this save anything or bring the System crashing to the ground? She didn't know, but she administered the special rations dutifully and watched as they were ravenously devoured.

Morana scrutinized her charge. If the Harvester was being truthful, this female would play an important role, and Morana must be able to distinguish her amongst an identical Herd. This one was starving, or sick. Maybe both. That could help. But mainly it was the eyes again, from which gleamed a pale yellow fire unlike anything Morana had ever seen. She felt sure she'd recognize them again.

The feeding over, Morana provided what medical care she could and sent her charge away with instructions to return in a month. She knew that meant nothing to someone who lived without time, but what else was she to say? If the Harvester was right, she'd get on the lists somehow, and they'd bring her back at the proper time. She gazed at the closed door through which her charge had disappeared, wondering what the future would bring.

Chapter Nine

"ALL AGAINST ALL—THAT'S THE FIRST STEP!" CHIEF TALEN drummed his fingers on the table as the squad members listened intently. "The Shock must distract, and to distract it must occupy the attention of all by turning them against all. How do we do that? By making them desire what the others have! By making them want to be what the others are!"

Drake raised his hand.

"But how can we make them want to imitate each other if they all look and act the same already? What's the point of imitating someone who's the same as you?"

Talen raised one long finger and held it aloft with impressive gravity.

"Ah, therein lies the problem, my boy—therein lies the problem! We must create or find differences to engender imitative desire."

Drake and his comrades frowned.

"I know what you're thinking," Talen continued with a wave of his hand. "Why resort to such measures? Won't they undo everything we've accomplished? The answer, in the first case, is because we must; in the latter, it's a resounding no. We must create the Shock to prevent boredom and the rebellion that will inevitably follow. It's simple mathematics. Bound to happen sometime or other. Might not even be a full revolt—perhaps just a minor . . . *disturbance*. But neither is acceptable. So, we create the Shock—turn them all against each other. This is done by creating small differences—just small ones, mind you!—that lead to the feelings just described. We give up a little to gain everything."

He grinned.

"We allow them to exhaust themselves in this universal strife, and then we end it."

"How?" Drake inquired.

"By turning the universal war into a war against just one."

"Which one?"

"Patience, lad!" exclaimed the laughing Chief as he wiped his brow. "Give your brain time to match your exuberance! It doesn't matter *which* one—just so long as there is *a* one. That's the key. The specifics can be resolved later. For now, merely understand what must occur."

The entire group nodded.

"Then order will be restored. The Herd, having vented its rage on the unfortunate *one*, will return to a state of grateful dependence on and submission to us Directors. Any questions?"

The solemn little group—perhaps a dozen or so in number—shook their heads.

"Good. Let's discuss the triggering events. We must move quickly. The Shock as a concept has been planned since the beginning, but the method of accomplishment remains largely unsettled. That's why you all are here. Some of the brightest and hungriest young Tithers have been assigned to this problem. I repeat—time is running short. We expect fast results, but don't act so fast things spiral completely out of control. Introduce differentiating features . . . *wisely!* Any suggestions?"

Again it was Drake who spoke.

"I just remembered! We use the one feature they don't all share—the one we haven't leveled yet!" he exclaimed.

Talen smiled. "Yes—*yes*, my boy! And explain to me how you will do it."

Chapter Ten

MORANA WAS SHOCKED AT THE STATE OF THE DISMAL apartment. Not that it was grungy or unclean; in fact, the place was immaculate—far more so than her own dwelling. It was the diminutive size that surprised her. The small rooms were smothered by ceilings so low she had to stoop under every doorframe. The tiny kitchen and dining area had taken scarcely a minute to examine, and she now stood in a slightly larger room that clearly served the dual purpose of living area and sleeping quarters.

Barney had taken a fortnight to contact her. She'd almost given up hope, thinking the Harvester had either taken fright or reported her. But then she'd received the note with an address and a time, only to show up and find no sign of her fellow conspirator.

The room contained no furniture save for a modest armchair, a delicate wood table, and a cot in the corner. The table and its intricately carved floral pattern delighted her, but strangely it was the large cassette player on top that drew her attention. She studied the machine, incongruous in its outmoded simplicity, and smiled. Reaching down, she playfully tapped the start button and was instantly transfixed by the resulting sound.

Two instrumental voices—strings and harpsichord working together in menacing symbiosis—began stalking toward her.

The melody was so sinister in tone that Morana could almost see it prowling around the machine, waiting to pounce. And pounce it did when a deep voice full of grim foreboding began with brooding intensity to send shivers of mixed terror and delight up Morana's spine. As she leaned forward, totally engrossed, the voice momentarily yielded to the instrumental accompaniment before returning once more, only to be cut off as a hand reached from behind her and hit pause. She whirled around.

Barney stood before her, his usually pale face so exceedingly blanched that Morana almost cried out. He gripped his Harvester cap so tightly in both hands that Morana could scarcely distinguish between the clenched, bone-colored fingers and the white scythe emblem showing against the dark background. They stared at each other.

"What are you doing, Miss?"

"I just turned on some music. It's been a while, you know!"

Morana laughed nervously as Barney remained silent. The terror returned.

"What darkness?" she whispered. "What darkness?"

He didn't answer, but he didn't need to. She could feel that darkness, or a manifestation of it, closing around her even now. An invisible darkness silently encircling her like a smothering fog. And this Harvester—would he really help her fight it?

"The darkness of the heart, Miss. The heart and the evil it contains—evil outlined in the entire book."

Morana jolted back to reality, stunned at the unexpected and enigmatic response.

"What? What evil . . . and what book?"

"One that no longer exists—it's forbidden."

"But reading isn't forbidden!" exclaimed Morana, growing bolder. "Not for Tithers! Nor is music, so why are you so—"

"Reading is not forbidden, provided you read what you're supposed to read. Things forbidden to read were removed some time ago. Same with music. The music you just played no longer exists—it's been erased. The only part left is what you hear twice daily."

"The Anthem?"

"Exactly. The music and the book that inspired it are expunged—they kept only the part deemed useful. Yet even that part they pervert in meaning. The mountains being made low refers not to physical objects razed but hearts prepared."

"Prepared for what?" Morana questioned eagerly. Her entire being longed for something she couldn't name. "The darkness?"

"No—the darkness is already there and has always been there."

"Where? The heart?"

"Yes."

"But not everyone's? Yours, for example, seems good."

"No, it's not. It's dark like everyone else's. So dark that I helped create the tyranny I just described. I wish I could say I'd simply been naive, but I can't. I knew it was wrong back then too. So did my wife, but she fought back and was harvested as a result. And now I've lived as a tool of the very system I despise, though ever since her fall I've sought the overthrow of that system. Still . . . in the meantime, so many have gone."

He shook his head. "She sang it too, you know."

"What?"

"The Anthem. There are female parts as well."

"It all makes sense! I knew I'd heard the Anthem somewhere, even if Dorg denied it! And this new part—I recognized that too, but only vaguely, as though through a haze. Let me hear the rest!" she pleaded.

A commotion at the entrance cut her short.

***

Four individuals emerged from the tiny entryway, all strangers. Barney introduced the single male figure as Max, a low-level admin among the Harvesters tasked with doctoring records and performing other necessary background work. Two females— Lorna and Kay by name—worked in the Calumny Bureau alongside Tempest, for whom they both displayed the utmost contempt. The final visitor led some obscure department she'd never heard of. Morana, her spirits lifted by this unexpected show of support, listened eagerly as the group's planning began.

After an hour, all she'd gleaned was the importance of her getting Shock information from Drake. The others had explained their responsibilities and how it impacted the overall plan, but Morana couldn't focus. Her initial relief at finding allies was overwhelmed by a feeling of complete insignificance amidst a machine that ground its opponents into submission. Don't worry, Barney told her. She was just to focus on her task. He'd get helpers within the Herd as well. So now she was headed home, guiltily awaiting Drake's next visit knowing her motives for seeing him were less than pure.

Still, so were his.

Chapter Eleven

BILLIE COULDN'T REMEMBER FEELING THIS GOOD. EVEN HER racking cough failed to dampen her spirits. She still lived in a timeless dream, but one with hope guiding her through the fog like a shining light.

She found hope amongst her fellow slaves as well. Clandestine glances at those around her revealed remnants of emotions and feelings on the faces of some. Others were clearly gone, mentally if not physically, but some . . . some were still *thinking*. A few times Billie had even seen that all-important spark of resentment in a pair of haggard eyes. Some would fight. And Barney was working on others—ones rescued from the Harvest and hidden away.

Even the recent changes failed to discourage her, though they had disproportionately affected her. Every day the loudspeakers now sang out the name of the single group that had proved the most deserving of freedom. No one questioned how equal slaves could be more or less *anything*— it was just so. Today had been Brown Group—one significantly larger than the others, even Blue Group, a concept which had initially failed to register in minds from which numbers had been erased. The loudspeakers began reminding them, however. It also reminded them that Green Group had delighted in despair better than their counterparts and that Hazel Group had stifled every genius in its infancy in a manner most pleasing to the Directors.

Billie found herself bounced from group to group, finally ending up in a small collection of oddities too unusual to make any larger group of their own. Even here, Billie proved exceptional—a misfit among misfits. She liked it. It gave her more freedom to work and even provided potential allies for her cause.

Yes—a movement was growing, and Billie could feel it. She could also feel a distended stomach, but that was no longer a problem. If nothing else, that fact alone gave her hope.

Chapter Twelve

MORANA HAD NO INFORMATION FROM DRAKE. SHE'D BARELY even seen him. He hadn't responded to her inquiries about the Shock squad, much to her surprise. She'd praised him and provided opportunities to brag about himself and his work as he always did, but he'd merely ignored her. She felt useless. Gathering intelligence on the Shock was her responsibility, and she had failed.

She knew it would be soon. Everyone talked about it, and several of her patients had a distinctly aggressive attitude, silent though they were. One had even stared her right in the face, though without animosity, an emotion she apparently reserved for another Herd birther nearby. It was strange.

She tried pressing Cozbi but unwisely mentioned Drake's taciturnity, something which her friend—once again Drake's lover, unbeknownst to Morana—promptly reported, thus destroying her ability to obtain information. Morana felt miserable, her only hope a vague plan which now seemed hopelessly unrealistic. Drake, moreover, was now beyond reach, even as a partner. She was alone.

While in this gloomy frame of mind, she received a summons to appear before the Superintendent.

***

Dorg wasn't smiling this time. The faint sneering upturn at one corner of the fine lips conveyed pure malice. The terrible eyes gleamed, and Morana instantly dropped hers before their trenchant gaze.

She entered and waited for him to speak first as before, but he remained silent, scrutinizing her intently. He stood leaning over the desk with his hands placed a little over shoulder width apart. Morana hesitated, then spoke.

"I've done as you commanded, sir. I have ceased acting selfishly and have instead taken upon myself the burden of directorship as you advised."

She paused and held her breath. To her astonishment, Dorg's entire frame began shaking—violently trembling with what Morana finally recognized as mute laughter. The beatific face twitched, and the Superintendent collapsed into his chair as though unable to support himself any longer. Morana stared.

"Pardon me, Ms. . . . uh, Ms. Morana . . . my dear! Oh! I apologize . . . you have amused me so greatly I . . . I can hardly respond! Her *burden*!" And he burst into peals of laughter so silent it seemed as though he would explode from the internalized energy such violent revelry must certainly engender. Morana was genuinely terrified and began backing away.

"Stay! Oh, do stay!" Dorg pleaded needlessly. He shook himself and grew calmer. "Do stay. We have much to discuss, and I'm glad we could start off with such great amusement as you have just provided."

"Me, sir? What did I say wrong?"

"Nothing, nothing! What you said was perfect, just perfect! That's exactly what I want you to say and how I want you to say it! You just had me fooled for a minute, as you said it so convincingly it almost sounded as though you actually believed it!"

"But I do, sir! I took to heart what you said last time, and I've implemented it as you directed! My numbers should be quite satisfactory!"

Dorg froze.

"I directed nothing, Ms. Morana."

"Sir?"

"I directed nothing. And all the nonsense I gave you about *burdens*, and *selfishness*, and *paradise*! Are you really saying you believed all that?"

"Yes, sir! I mean . . . yes, I believe you, but no . . . not if . . . that is, I believe you, but if you were joking, then I don't believe what you said." Morana writhed with confused despair.

"I was not joking."

"Yes, sir. But . . . I thought . . . you just said—"

"I believe another lecture is in order, my dear. You operate by extremes, Ms. Morana. On the one hand, you take literally what I tell you, and on the other, you say I'm joking. Neither is correct. I was certainly not joking, but neither should my comments have been taken literally. The spiel I gave you is not a joke, it's reality; but it's reality as seen by the Herd. In other words, it's what *they* must believe. They must believe you to be acting in their best interests. They must believe you to be a model of selfless sacrifice ushering in the state of perfectly free despotism characterizing the future earthly paradise. A paradise they must, of course, believe in.

"We, however, need not believe in it—in fact, doing so is both naive and damaging to the System and other Tithers.

The fate of the Herd is incidental, their happiness dispensable. The only reason we care at all is because a dissatisfied Herd is one that will rebel, and that would be most inconvenient to our goal. You know what the goal is, Ms. Morana?"

"The paradise?"

"NO!" Dorg almost screamed, springing from his chair and leaning toward the shrinking Leveler. "No! The paradise is what we promise to keep them submissive, but that is not the goal! The goal is our enjoyment, our pleasure—that of the Directors, the Tithers. That is and has always been our aim, our only aim! Damn the Herd! What I said previously is correct—we can't get rid of them, so we keep them and tell them it's for their own good. But don't *ever* believe that yourself!"

He paused, wiped his sweatless brow, and grinned.

"After all, we are gougers, not acolytes! We trick, not indoctrinate! The only doctrine a Tither should hold is that which abhors all doctrine. Never be taken in—that's the key! That, and doing whatever is necessary to maximize our own pleasure.

"Tithers are not great as such. What makes us great and separates us from the Herd is that we separated the Herd from us. We are great because we say we are and then act on that belief. If Tithers were great in and of themselves, no leveling would be required, for all slaves would be stupid and all Tithers brilliant. But you can see this isn't the case! Many of the Herd are quite intelligent and must be leveled or even harvested, and some Tithers are so witless they can scarcely hold a conversation. So, clearly, Tithers are not Tithers because they are naturally biologically superior across the board! No, Tithers direct because we gained the right to do so simply by declaring the right to do so . . . and then in fact doing so! And the fact that the Herd *allowed* us to do so confirms for all eternity the right to subjugate them, and to do so *scientifically*.

"Your friend Cozbi claims we lack scientific capabilities. She speaks again out of a childish—though loyal—ignorance. We have great scientific capabilities, many of which we Tithers use for our own benefit. We have simply determined—scientifically!—that science and its benefits should be reserved for us and us alone. Why waste scientific effort slowly improving the lives of billions when those resources can instead be devoted to our own well-being? Moreover, how could scientific benefits be applied *equally* to those billions? An impossible task! We tried, and it simply became too cumbersome. The question is not about capabilities, but rather our wisdom in applying them. Our capabilities are vast, but our discretion is even greater. We have enough science—what we need is rigid discipline for the masses! What is Slogan Four?"

"Down with culture!" Morana blurted mechanically.

"Exactly! Down with it all—for the masses, that is! *We* can have beautiful music, art, and literature—providing it furthers System principles—but the Herd must do without, for any attempt to benefit from it would harm the state of purest equality they enjoy. Disparity in beauty necessitates equality of ugliness. Say a great scientist makes a discovery—he is now elevated above the rest of the Herd! A great musician a symphony—his talent becomes exceptional! An artist's masterpiece separates him from those who can't paint, and a writer's magnum opus shatters the spirit of universal leveling which makes all equal. And since we cannot have *all* Herd members making scientific discoveries or creating works of art, *none* of them can be allowed to do so. Tithers, meanwhile, can engage in these activities to their hearts' content. *All* activities."

Dorg's calm smile suddenly morphed into a look of such malevolent concentration that Morana nearly shrieked. The perfect nose was gone, replaced by nostrils flaring so expansively they seemed poised to envelop the entire face in their gaping blackness. The eyes shot flames. In an instant, the desk no longer separated them, and Morana found herself backing away as Dorg advanced, his entire frame twitching.

"All activities, all pleasures, are ours!" he snarled. "All! But now the Herd—in their leveled state—can't fulfill certain pleasures. What use have I for females who look like males? None! But you . . . *you!* I need you!"

Morana screamed and turned to flee but was grabbed from behind by an icy grip of steel. She swooned, and everything went black.

Chapter Thirteen

THE RAGE IN MORANA'S HEAVING CHEST NEARLY SMOTHERED her. Only the gasping sobs undermined a feeling of invincible power sweeping over her. All restraint thrown aside, she would stop at nothing to take the System down.

She hit her head on the doorframe and paused to collect herself. Barney had sent her here, but for what? He had sprung into action after grimly listening to her story. They had to move fast—Dorg's act made haste imperative. He might keep her as a mistress, but more likely he'd have her harvested. His type always grew disgusted with themselves and attacked the objects of their past desire. Her time was limited—even now he probably regretted letting her go. She'd come . . . for the papers. Yes, the papers! The ones Max had prepared. To get them while Barney gathered his secret forces from places only he knew. But she knew the apartment and the empty space under the floor.

Morana found the cache with no difficulty but stopped as she withdrew the illicit documents. A small bundle of papers, separate from the rest and covered in tiny, penciled script, lay enclosed in an unmarked plastic bag. She grabbed this packet along with the rest, replaced the floorboard, and hurried away, halting once again in front of the machine. She couldn't resist playing it.

That same deep voice cried out to her from depths

unknown, yet this time it was hopeful, expectant! Morana began crying, unsure whether terror or joy prevailed in her stricken heart. Where was it? She knew the darkness, but where was this light? Trembling with emotions so convoluted she scarcely knew how to react, she flew toward the entranceway and straight into a warm body. She screamed.

"My apologies."

The speaker looked down at her and smiled. "I'm the manager—just stopped by to see Barney. May I ask your name? And what's that you're listening to?"

Morana gasped. In her ecstatic state she'd forgotten to turn off the music.

"Oh, hi! I'm Morana! I'm a friend of Barney's, and he just asked me to grab some stuff for him." She transferred her slim attaché case to a nonchalant position under her shaking arm. "I was just listening to some of his music."

The man cocked his head to one side, listening. "What baleful stuff!"

"It wasn't so dark a moment ago," Morana retorted, feeling strangely defensive. "The timbre keeps changing from scary to . . . not scary. Not happy exactly, but triumphant. Yes, that's it!" she exclaimed with satisfaction. "It's triumphant, but in a sort of expectant way, like something bad is happening now but won't last forever!"

The man regarded her silently, and his polite, unwavering smile began to discomfit her.

"I'll leave now—just let me lock up," she prompted.

The smile widened. "These rooms don't lock—none of them do."

Morana winced. "That's right—well, I'll just turn it off and leave. I'll let him know you stopped by."

She slipped back into the room momentarily before returning to the passageway. The man backed slowly out the door, bowing slightly as he did so.

"Well, goodbye!"

Morana fled down the stairs, leaving her unwelcome visitor alone.

***

She ran toward her own apartment but found three Harvesters waiting outside the building entrance. They'd come for her already. She darted down a side street and tried to think.

Where could she go? Not home, and not back to Barney's. They'd be after him soon, if she'd judged that manager right. She didn't know where the others lived, and soon her face would trigger every camera from the hilltop to the Enclosure. The Enclosure! She might go unnoticed there. Morana directed her rapid steps toward the Herd.

The gates stood wide open, no sentries present. Hiding her face as much as possible, she passed through and plowed straight into the heart of the vast uniformity before her. Something felt different. Before she could determine the source of the low rumbling sound reaching her ears, she noticed a large group of Tithers heading up a parallel street toward the gates. Morana watched as this force disappeared inside the ramparts and emerged moments later atop the wall, spreading out like so many ants upon a log. Morana now observed the entire wall, as far as the eye could see in both directions, lined with Tithers watching the vast landscape beneath them. What was happening? Morana felt exposed and darted behind another building. Why had they abandoned the Enclosure, and what were those ever-increasing noises?

She suddenly felt watched and looked wildly around. A pair of frightened gray eyes peered at her from around the corner.

"Who are you?" she whispered.

The female slave made no reply but slid into full view and stood before her, shaking.

"Who are you?" Morana repeated.

"Help." The reply came in a flat monotone, as though the speaker had long since lost the power of articulation.

"Help you? But what's wrong? And how can you possibly trust me?"

The trembling automaton remained mute.

Morana tried to think. Something was wrong. This slave feared a Leveler less than her own kind. The unusual gray eyes, round with terror, gave no answer to the riddle, but Morana recognized her opportunity.

"Here! Take my clothes—I'll trade you! You put on mine, and I'll put on yours. You can disappear, and I'll just blend in with the Herd, which is what I wanted anyway. Okay?"

No response. Morana, growing more frenzied as the chaotic hubbub increased in volume, removed her own clothes and then began tearing the uniform from the androgynous form before her. She threw on the stinking garments and stuffed the papers from her case down the front of her shirt, trying with shaking hands to dress her counterpart but was only halfway through before a solid mass of figures emerged from around a nearby street corner. The slave shrieked and ran headlong in the direction of the gates, her unbuttoned garments streaming behind her. As Morana stood undecided, the mob began running toward her with loud, indistinct shouts. She was soon surrounded by slaves peering intently into her face, mere inches away, a few even grabbing her head and holding it as they stared with terrifying intensity into her startled eyes. The vague and disjointed noises soon morphed into distinguishable cries of "Blue, blue!" which reverberated along the street. They released Morana, who immediately felt herself swept up in an irresistible flow of bodies. As she ran, trying to avoid getting trampled, she noticed countless others converging into one solid mass, like tiny rivulets merging into a mighty river of human flesh. They ran with a noise like the humming of a giant machine, and Morana gasped for air as she tried desperately to keep up. She felt her knees buckle, and she managed to stagger sideways before collapsing against a wall where she lay motionless.

***

She came to with head throbbing and ears ringing. Staggering to her feet, she trudged through the deserted streets toward the distant tumult, a mysterious force drawing her onward.

It took an age to reach the massive square before the Spire, now densely covered in a solid mass of human forms. Morana fought her way toward the monolith, unable to see more than a few yards ahead but somehow certain she must reach this structure. Her entire body ached with pain and fatigue, but she pushed forward until the tower's twenty stories rose almost directly above her and she reached a small open space formed by the wide steps leading up to the abandoned entrance. Atop these steps a handful of slaves surrounded a bloodied, naked figure who lay gasping upon the pavement, her frail arms extended toward a tiny screaming bundle lying nearby.

Chapter Fourteen

MORANA'S FATIGUE VANISHED AS SHE WATCHED THE SLAVES drag this tortured victim up and down the bloody steps. A feeling of helpless, impotent rage overwhelmed her, and she rushed forward and scooped up the child and the garments in which he lay. She flew at the brutish thugs, screaming at them to stop, but they merely stared at her with unhinged malignance. It was only when she knelt beside the moaning female that Morana noticed the bright yellow eyes now dimmed with approaching death. She gasped.

"It's her!" she whispered. "I'll help you! I'll help!"

But at that moment she was struck so forcefully from behind that she fell and almost crushed her precious bundle. The slaves dragged the hapless mother through the tower doors, leaving Morana to scramble to her feet and scurry after them, the child swaddled and hidden in her arms.

Upon entering, Morana paused. This child was not safe. She looked desperately for a hiding place and observed a small room off to the side into which she darted and placed the screaming child, then climbed the narrow stairs after the slaves and their ghastly burden. Her strength almost failed her, and she emerged onto the open observation platform only to fall to her knees, gasping for breath.

Billie's mutilated form knelt before the railing, her head sunk forward, and two slaves held her body upright. Morana could hear a mighty roar from below. She staggered to her feet and approached the edge.

The enormity of the horde below was shocking. Not only the square but every bit of pavement writhed with human forms, all directing their crazed eyes upward. She remained motionless, thunderstruck. Here stood the Herd in all its grotesque reality, eyes inflamed by some contagion and garbled voices resounding to the very heavens. And then the roar redoubled its fury as Morana turned to find Billie held aloft and cast over the railing into the cauldron of human flesh.

Morana never heard the impact, drowned by the furor of voices which reached a dizzying pitch. She collapsed to a sitting position and sobbed, holding her knees.

***

It was over. The masses had dispersed, the tumult ceased. Morana slowly descended the stairs and took the child in her arms. Clasping him to her breast, she felt the papers under her shirt.

All through the long night she read the contents of the mysterious packet, Max's documents lying forgotten on the floor. Page after page, she strained to make out the tiny script painstakingly copied by hand onto the wafer-thin sheets of paper. She wept and she laughed, even mouthing words with closed eyes to imprint them upon her mind forever.

The child was dying, and daylight brought a surreal mixture of joy and sorrow. As Morana sat contemplating, the door suddenly opened.

Tempest stood blinking in the doorway. The two regarded

each other in mute astonishment before the intruder broke the silence.

"There you are. They were looking for you back there." She waved vaguely.

"I know. And I suppose you'll be desperate to help them find me."

Tempest tossed her head. "Why should I be? They all think I'm stupid." She laughed. "They're all in a fit—some big conspiracy they barely caught in time. That's probably why they haven't gone through the footage yet and picked you up. Anyway, how'd you get here, and in that uniform? Looks like the Shock went exactly how they wanted. I think—"

"Tempest."

The urgency in Morana's voice cut Tempest's ramblings short.

"I need help. Are you going to turn me in or not?"

"I have to. The others are right behind me. I'm only the first one here—came to get some records."

"Can't you just say you didn't see me? Let me blend back in with the slaves if they're peaceful again."

"Oh, they're peaceful, alright! Quite ready to follow commands now that their golden-eyed goddess has ended the plague. But you?" Tempest snickered. "How would *you* blend in? Just look at yourself!"

Morana froze as the reality of her situation finally hit her. How *could* she blend in? She, with her beautiful hair, shapely figure, and unblemished face? What had she been thinking this whole time? She looked nothing like the Herd, nor they her. She sank into a chair and covered her face with her hands. At that moment, the child began coughing faintly. Tempest gasped.

"An offspring! Where'd you get it? I didn't even see it. It sounds terrible—what's the matter with it? And what were you planning on doing with it?"

An idea began to form in Morana's mind.

"You take him."

Tempest looked confused.

"Take him . . . and take these." She stuffed the papers into Tempest's hands.

"I can't stand the nasty little things! It's a slave too, isn't it? That's even worse!"

"It'll be worth your while."

"How so?" Tempest asked, intrigued.

"Don't worry—I've got it all figured out. And don't lose those papers."

Chapter Fifteen

"AH, THERE YOU ARE!" DORG CROONED AS HE ENTERED. Morana leapt to her feet, eyes blazing.

"Oh, don't worry!" the silky drawl advised. "I have no interest in you personally—find you rather disgusting, frankly. I've come to talk business."

"What business?" Morana spat the words with such vehemence that Dorg laughed.

"Well, aren't we fiery now? Quite a change from the trembling little Leveler. The business of justice, Ms. Morana. You have sabotaged the System, and the System demands justice."

Morana stood silent, shaking with rage. She recoiled at the thought of groveling before this monster and wanted to rip him apart with her bare hands, but she determined to carry out her plan.

"No! Spare me, at least for a little while!"

Dorg smiled. "The bravery sure didn't last long. And why should you be granted a reprieve, however temporary?"

"Because I'm pregnant!" Morana announced. She held her breath and watched as Dorg's face blanched, flushed, then grew white again as surprise, shame, and finally anger dominated his countenance. She targeted his vanity.

"It's a boy—I know it is! He'll be a great leader. You can raise him for power. His genetics will be unmatched—you know I'm more beautiful and intelligent than any woman you'll find. I already found someone to raise him, so you'll never have to care for him. Just wait until he's born, then do what you want with me."

She watched the Superintendent's eyes spark.

"As you wish. You've given me an idea—a special plan just for you. The timing should work perfectly, given our projections. But I don't want to see him until he's grown. If he's superior, I'll claim him—if not, he'll follow you to the Harvest. You'll live in complete yet comfortable seclusion until you give birth, at which point your health no longer matters."

Dorg turned, then paused. "Oh, I almost forgot to mention— black's the new color!"

"Black?"

"Yes, that's the new color for the Herd. They're all going to have black eyes. We can do that, you know. I told you we had scientific capabilities!" He chuckled. "Well, so long, my dear! Say hello to your friend for me!"

***

Morana's escort opened the cell door and disappeared. She found Barney lying face upward on the bare floor, his chest heaving with a rattling sound more terrible than the clanking of the shackles on his lacerated limbs. His bloody clothing clung to him like shredded paper. Morana barely recognized a face swollen to gigantic proportions and crowned with hair now uniformly gray, though speckled with red.

She knelt over the dying Harvester, crying softly. "I found the light," she whispered.

Barney smiled faintly.

"I found it, and the darkness has not overcome it."

A harsh grating sound and the door opened again, a hulking form completely blocking the passage behind. Grub stood leering like a bloated, uniformed grave worm, his fingers twitching on the ends of his short arms like fat tendrils on some strangely blanched and swollen sea creature. Enveloping her in his rotting embrace, he dragged her from the room.

Chapter Sixteen

"THE CEREMONY WILL TAKE PLACE TOMORROW."

Morana surveyed the dumpy little woman in the rumpled pantsuit sitting before her and tried to focus. The droning monotone reminded her of insects buzzing.

"What ceremony?"

"The Harvesting—the celebration of the Harvest Tenfold." The tone of bland dullness implied obvious certainty impossible to misinterpret.

"But what role do I play?"

The woman heaved a sigh as though disgusted at Morana's simplicity.

"You're the final Harvest. Well, not the last one . . . we continue as before, but we've met our initial goal."

"What goal?"

"A billion. You're number one billion. The numbers won't technically be exact, as we're collecting data from so many Threshing Centers worldwide, but it's close enough."

"But . . . I don't understand."

"You don't have to. Just follow instructions. You'll be brought forward, speeches will be made, and you'll be presented to the Grand Despot."

"The Grand Despot will be there?"

"Yes, of course I will."

Morana stared.

"That's all." The woman made a quick note in her binder, rose from her chair, and left the room.

***

Grub's face twisted with murderous rage, but Morana no longer feared him. This living hell was over. Her "pregnancy" complete, he had his orders. No longer could he benefit from her supposed condition. No longer could he laugh in her face like when she'd threatened to confess her lie and end this nightmare by embracing immediate death. He'd simply threatened to kill the child and report Tempest. These two were the only living beings she'd seen for a year, and both now shared her secret—the one receiving a generous stipend from Dorg for the raising of a child he'd never met, and the other loathe to reveal a deception which could now only implicate himself as well. He'd had his fun, but now the Harvest had come.

The ceremony was merely a blur of speeches, lights, cameras, and noise. Morana, her senses dulled, felt like she was drowning or falling, except now it would finally end. She didn't care about the ceremony, even if billions were watching. Let them watch. She'd soon be free.

The Harvesting flitted by like a dream. A room, a list, commands; a vehicle, a journey, mountains. After the mountains, a vast wasteland. A wasteland with countless living and countless dead. "But the Harvest?" she asked. "How am I killed?" They laughed. What were they, barbarians? They rarely *negated* anyone. It was more efficient, more scientific, to simply let the Harvest wither. Assign resources equally—to those deemed worthy, of course. Those remaining . . . well, they'd be equal in lack thereof.

They smiled, and then they left.

Epilogue

A YOUTH OF RUDDY COUNTENANCE AND NOBLE DEMEANOR surveys the mighty throng with eyes of purest gold. He watches the ritual sacrifice brought forth and listens to the proclamations made. He watches the marble icon with its painted yellow orbs hurtle downward and shatter to dust amidst a mighty roar. He listens as he who dares call him son pronounces him a living god, one who carries the same fire in his eyes as her they made divine. He watches, listens, and remembers.

He remembers a greater sacrifice—one sufficient for all time. He remembers the light that shines in the darkness. He remembers, and he plans.

For one day he will end this pageantry, this mockery of freedom. He will exchange their bondage for true slavery—the slavery that brings true freedom. And he will reap a harvest—a harvest hundredfold.

Acknowledgements

Many thanks to Kath, Erika, and Catherine for your fantastic work on this project!

Dostoevsky, you mad genius—my warnings can hardly succeed where yours have failed, but at least we can say we tried. Please excuse my stealing ideas and lines from your characters to create a fun little story. I hope I did it justice.

"To him who sits on the throne and to the Lamb be blessing and honor and glory and might forever and ever!"

About the Author

An avid reader, Bahr Burr's interest in creating the written word continues to grow as required college writing assignments fade into the merciful oblivion of forgotten memories. Bahr explores themes of human nature and moral agency in his reading and writing journey. His favorite author is Dostoevsky.

A native Texan, Bahr enjoys eating meat and watching rugby, ideally simultaneously.

Subscribe to The Bahr Burr Project on Substack for more of Bahr's literary endeavors.